The Treasure

Written by Jill Eggleton
Illustrated by Jim Storey

Rigby

Here is the map.

Here is the rock.

4

No treasure!

Here is the tree.

6

No treasure!

Here is the cave.

No treasure!

Here is the hole.

13

A Map

▰▰ Guide Notes

Title: The Treasure
Stage: Emergent – Magenta

Genre: Fiction
Approach: Guided Reading
Processes: Thinking Critically, Exploring Language, Processing Information
Visual Focus: Map

READING THE TEXT

Tell the children that the story is about pirates who are looking for treasure.
Talk to them about what is on the front cover. Read the title and the author / illustrator.
"Walk" through the book, focusing on the illustrations and talking to the children about
the different things the pirates find instead of treasure.
Before looking at pages 12-13, ask the children to make a prediction.
Read the text together.

THINKING CRITICALLY
(sample questions)
- How do you think the jelly beans got in the box?
- What do you think the pirates could do with the jelly beans?

EXPLORING LANGUAGE
(ideas for selection)

Terminology
Title, cover, author, illustrator, illustrations

Vocabulary
Interest words: map, rock, treasure, tree, cave, hole, jelly beans
High-frequency words: here, is, the, no

Print Conventions
Capital letter for sentence beginnings, periods